KOREAN WORD BOOK

Marshall R. Pihl

Illustrated by
Roxanne Carrington

Bess Press
P.O. Box 22388
Honolulu, Hawaii 96823

Library of Congress Catalog Card Number 93-73161

Pihl, Marshall R.
Korean Word Book
Honolulu, Hawaii: The Bess Press, Inc.
112 pages

Second printing 1996
Hardcover ISBN: 1-880188-53-8
Paperback ISBN: 1-880188-52-X
Copyright © 1994 by The Bess Press, Inc.

CONTENTS

Introduction

There are 70 million Koreans on Earth. While 65 million live on the Korean peninsula, another five million live in 106 other countries, with 1.1 million in the United States. Koreans in the United States constituted only one per cent of all Asians in the population of the early 1950s but, due to constant immigration and natural increase, they have become the fastest growing group among Asian Americans. They now already outnumber Japanese and are predicted to be second only to Filipinos by the year 2030.

This amazing growth is traced back to the Civil Rights Act of 1964, which eliminated discrimination based on ethnicity and country of origin, and the Immigration Law of 1968, which eliminated discriminatory quotas that had been imposed on Asians. With these and other changes in American public policy, we have begun to move away from the "melting-pot" concept and toward a multicultural society in which Anglo-Saxon dominance must yield to a situation in which many different ethnicities are accepted and respected.

Koreans have been rapidly building a social, political, and economic power in America. Many Koreans are highly successful professionally and financially and there are many Korean professors, medical doctors, lawyers, engineers, certified public accountants, musicians, artists, politicians, and businessmen in America.

And now, with the social and industrial miracle of South Korea leading to its emergence as a significant world power and with the huge political and economic portents of imminent unification, we find that Koreans in the United States are taking deeper pride in their ethnicity and also that many non-Koreans are showing increasing interest in Korean culture, business, and products. It is therefore no accident that Korean Studies are rapidly expanding at colleges and universities throughout the country. Whereas only eleven universities offered a Korean program in 1971, the number has trebled in the past two decades. At present, some thirteen hundred students in thirty universities are enrolled in Korean programs.

The Korean language belongs to a group of languages, called "Altaic," that covers a wide band reaching from Turkey on the west to Japan on the east. Altaic languages share two major characteristics that make them different from English: the order of their words and the method they use to build up words. While English sentences have the order subject-verb-object ("man bites dog"), Altaic langauges put the verb at the end of the sentence ("man dog bites"). Furthermore, Altaic languages can add many endings to a word to mark its style or grammatical role in the sentence. One such ending is -yo, which is used in this book; it is added to change a word from intimate to polite style.

The 231 entries in this *Korean Word Book* represent the most commonly used words in the Korean langauge and their selection was based upon word frequency studies published by the Korean Ministry of Education, earlier word books published by Bess Press, and common sense. There are some high-frequency words that were not included in this book because their abstract nature did not lend itself easily to the artful but realistic illustrations created by Roxanne Carrington.

—Marshall R. Pihl

The editor of the *Korean Word Book,* Marshall R. Pihl, is a graduate of Seoul National University (M.A.) and Harvard University (A.B., Ph.D.). He has taught Korean language and literature at Harvard and Columbia and is now Associate Professor of Korean Literature at the University of Hawai‘i at Mānoa. His many publications include *Listening to Korea* (Praeger, 1973), *The Good People* (Heinemann, 1985), and *The Korean Singer of Tales* (Harvard, 1994). Dr. Pihl, who is president of the International Korean Literature Association, is currently preparing a comprehensive history of Korean literature for college students.

Roxanne Carrington, an illustrator living in Washington state, has lived in Korea and is a longtime student of Korean language and culture. She and her husband are adoptive parents of two Korean children, whom they encourage to maintain close ties with their heritage.

Pronunciation

There are about 30 sounds in the Korean language. Many of them are the same as in English; some are a little different; and a few must be newly learned. The major difference that distinguishes Korean and English pronunciation lies in the contrasts between groups of sounds. Whereas English has a two-way contrast between "voiceless sounds" (*p, t, k, ch, f, s,* etc.) and "voiced sounds" (*b, d, g, j, v, z,* etc.), Korean has a three-way contrast between "plain sounds" (*p, t, k, ch,* etc.), "reinforced sounds" (*pp, tt, kk, tch,* etc.), and "aspirated sounds" (*p', t', k', ch',* etc.). Thus, whereas English will distinguish between *pull* and *bull,* Korean distinguishes between *pul* "fire," *ppul* "horn," and *p'ul* "grass."

The plain sounds are rather like their English counterparts; the aspirated sounds require an extra puff of air (the apostrophe, as in *p'ul* "grass," helps you remember); and the reinforced sounds, written with double letters, require a tightening of the throat muscles (a glottal stop) when pronounced. To get an idea of aspiration, hold a small sheet of paper close in front of your lips and loudly say "pop" and "spin"; a puff of air will push the sheet when you say "pop" but it will stay still when you say "spin." That is because the *p* in "pop" is more heavily aspirated. Sometimes even English speakers use reinforcement to distinguish between words: *hot tea* and *haughty* would sound the same if it weren't for the reinforced *tt* in *hot tea.* In addition to these characteristics, we should note a small change that occurs to the plain sounds when they get caught between vowels (or vowel-like sounds): *p, t, k, ch* become temporarily voiced and pronounced as *b, d, g, j.* Therefore, you will find that we frequently use the letters *b, d, g, j* in the words we present in this book (as in *agi* "baby").

There are three Korean vowels for which the English alphabet lacks letters. In these cases we use letters from the International Phonetic Alphabet: ə as the *u* in "but," æ as the *a* in "bat," and ʉ as the *oo* in "look."

The Korean Alphabet

The Koreans use an alphabet which was created by a board of scholars in 1443. This remarkable script, called *hangʉl,* is the first alphabet in the world which was created on the basis of a scientific, phonemic analysis of a language. Furthermore, the consonant letters were given shapes based upon the appearance of the organs of articulation. For example, the letters ㄱ (*k*) and ㄴ (*n*) are stylized cross-section outlines of the tongue as it is positioned to make the two sounds. There are five basic consonant letters from which all others are derived. The shapes of the vowel letters were originally based on three basic marks (ㅣ , ㅡ, ㅇ), chosen to represent humankind, earth, and heaven respectively. Korean letters are grouped into syllabic clusters in which they are in a manner similar to a tic-tac-toe symbol. Thus, the word *hangʉl,* for example, is written in the following fashion: 한글, where 하 (*ha*) is written above ㄴ (*n*) and 그 (*gʉ*) is written above ㄹ (*l*). Had this been strung out in English style, the result would have looked like ㅎ ㅏ ㄴ ㄱ ㅡ ㄹ . When there is no initial consonant, it is replaced by the letter ㅇ as in 아기 (*agi*) "baby."

Consonant Letters							Vowel Letters							
ㄱ	ㄴ	ㄷ	ㄹ	ㅁ	ㅂ	ㅅ	ㅏ	ㅑ	ㅓ	ㅕ	ㅗ	ㅛ	ㅜ	ㅠ
k,g	n	t,d	r,l	m	p,b	s	a	ya	ə	yə	o	yo	u	yu
ㅇ	ㅈ	ㅊ	ㅋ	ㅌ	ㅍ	ㅎ	ㅡ	ㅣ	ㅢ	ㅐ	ㅒ	ㅔ	ㅖ	ㅚ
ng	ch,j	ch'	k'	t'	p'	h	ʉ	i	ʉi	æ	yæ	e	ye	oe
ㄲ	ㄸ	ㅃ	ㅆ	ㅉ			ㅘ	ㅙ	ㅟ	ㅝ	ㅞ			
kk	tt	bb	ss	tch			wa	wæ	wi	wə	we			

cha-yo

kkæ-yo

pada-yo

chuǝ-yo

ka-yo

wa-yo

urǝ-yo

usǝ-yo

sænggak hæ-yo

ssǝ-yo

tɰrǝ-yo

pwa-yo

tada-yo

yǝrǝ-yo

sǝ-yo

anja-yo

tallyǝ ga-yo

kǝrǝ ga-yo

ttwiǝ-yo

il hæ-yo

nora-yo

t'a-yo

na ga-yo

tɰrǝ ga-yo

shijak hæ-yo

mach'yǝ-yo

tora-yo

olla ga-yo

næryǝ ga-yo

ssisǝ-yo

sarang hæ-yo

ACTION

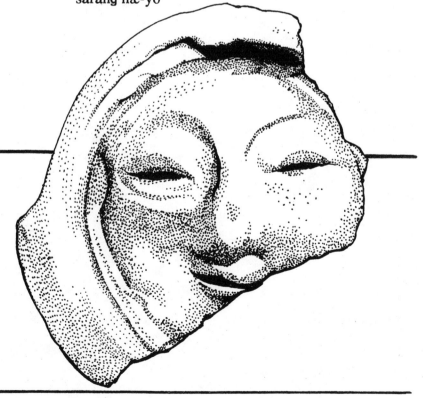

자요　　cha-yo

sleep

깨요

kkæ-yo

wake

받아요
pada-yo
receive

주어요
chuə-yo
give

가요   ka-yo

go

와요   wa-yo

come

울어요　　 urə-yo

cry

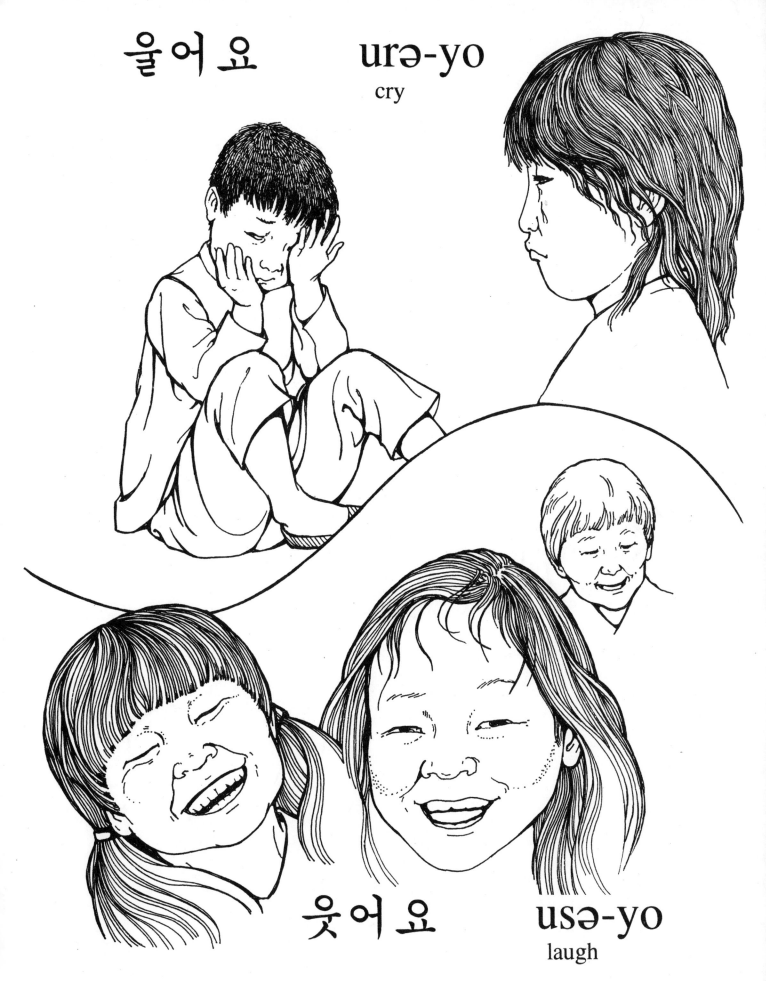

웃어요　　usə-yo

laugh

5

생각해요

sænggak hæ-yo

think

써요

ssə-yo

write

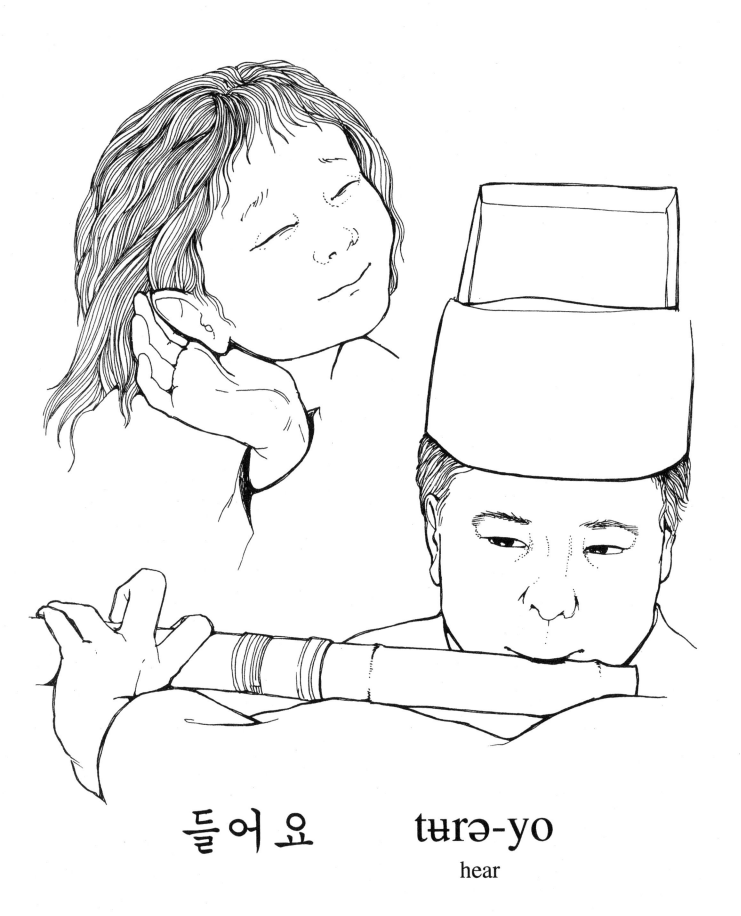

들어요   tɯrə-yo

hear

8

봐요

pwa-yo

see

9

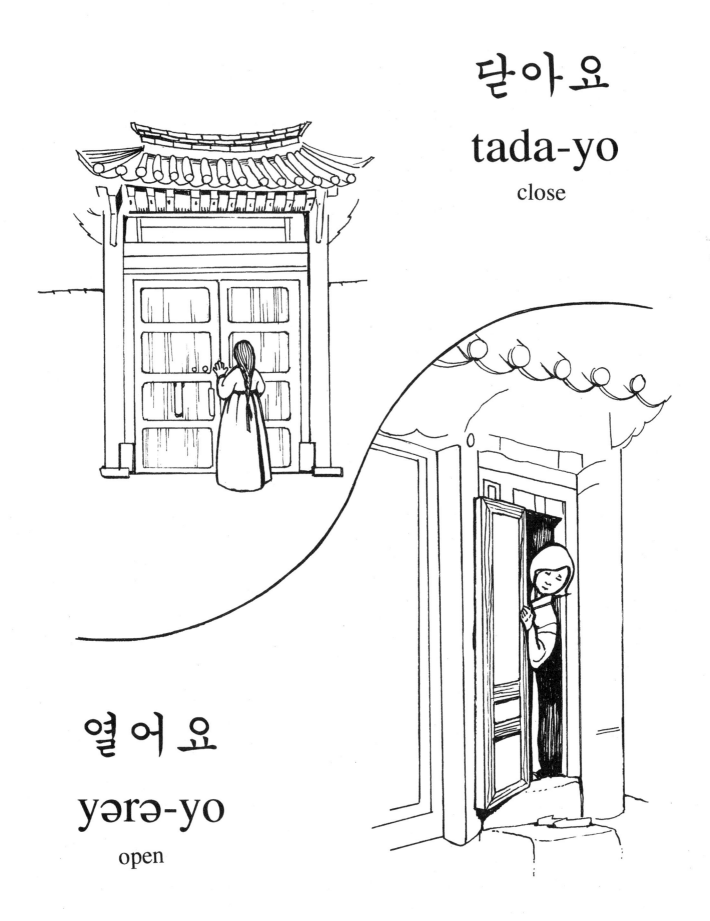

닫아요
tada-yo
close

열어요
yərə-yo
open

10

서요

sə-yo

stand

앉아요

anja-yo

sit

11

달려가요　tallyə ga-yo　run

걸어가요
kərə ga-yo
walk

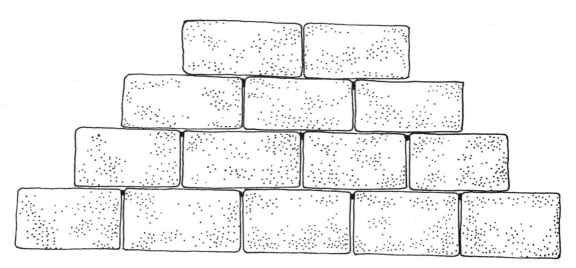

뛰어요　　　ttwiə-yo

jump

일 해 요　　il hæ-yo

work

14

놀아요

nora-yo

play

타요

t'a-yo

ride

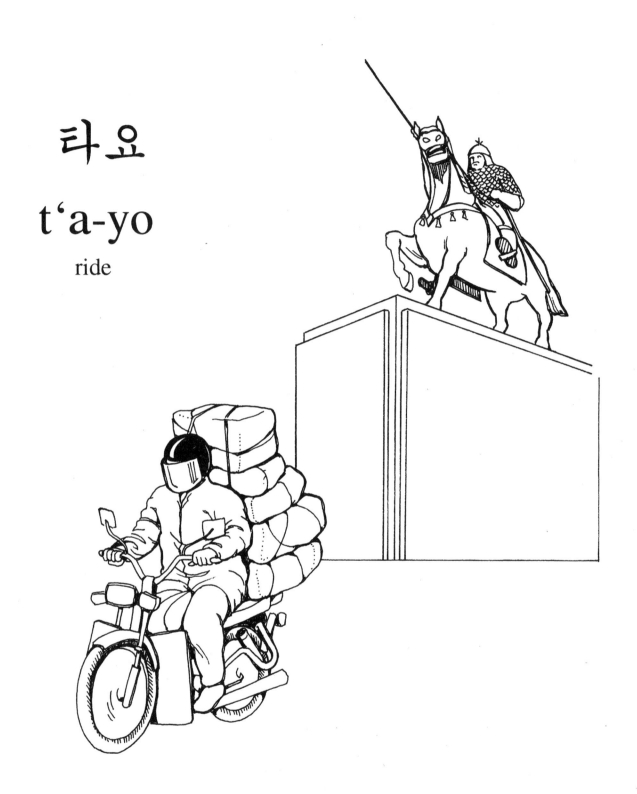

나가요   na ga-yo   go out

들어가요

tɰrə ga-yo

go in

시작해요 shijak hæ-yo
start

마쳐요
mach'yə-yo
finish

돌아요　　tora-yo

turn

올라가요 내려가요

olla
ga-yo

go up

næryə
ga-yo

go down

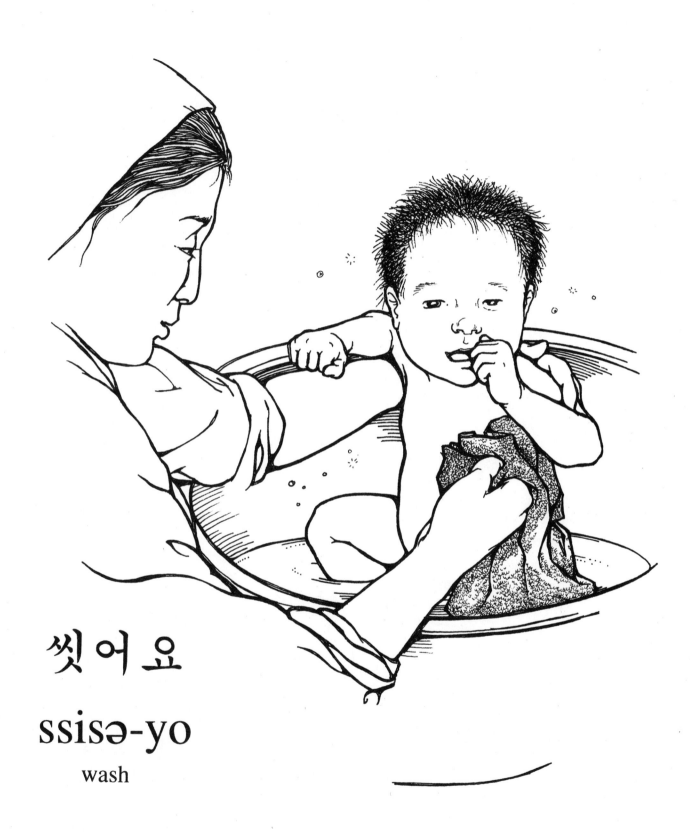

씻어요

ssisə-yo

wash

사랑해요　sarang hæ-yo

love

əlgul

t'əl	son karak	məri
nun	son t'op	kasɨm
kwi	him	əkkæ
nun-mul	tɨng	p'al
k'o	tari	son
ip	kungdungi	pæ
kogæ	murɨp	pæ kkop
t'ək	pal	mom

BODY

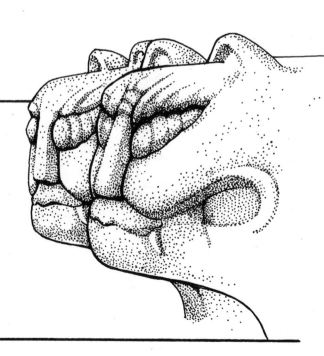

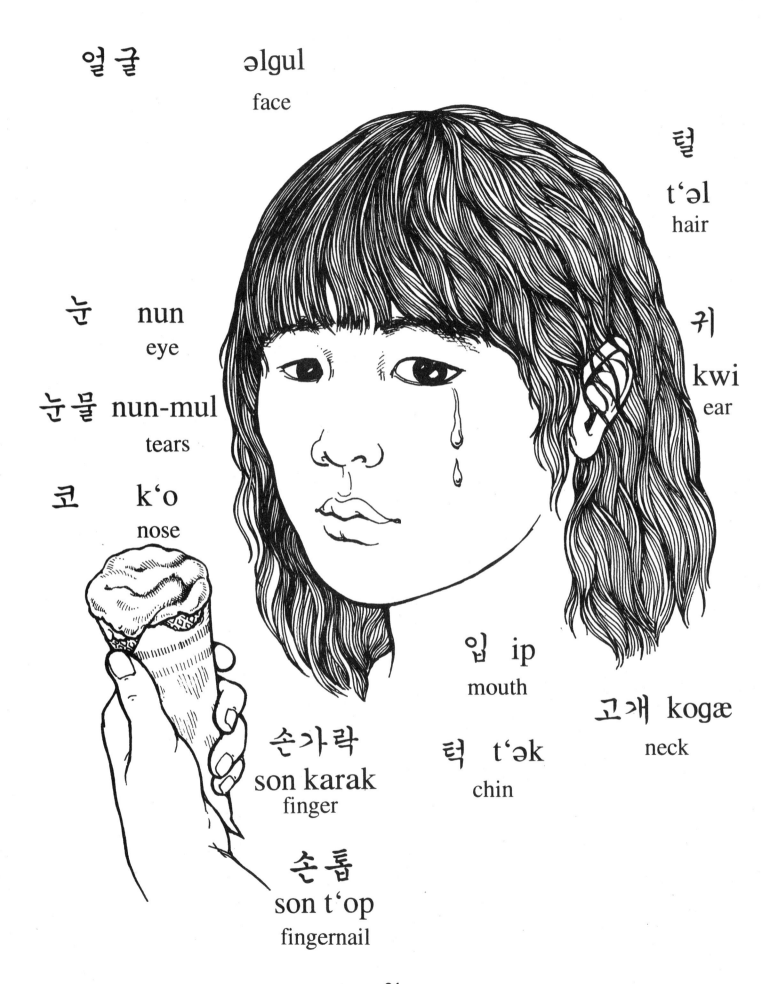

얼굴 əlgul
face

털 t'əl
hair

눈 nun
eye

눈물 nun-mul
tears

코 k'o
nose

귀 kwi
ear

입 ip
mouth

고개 kogæ
neck

손가락 son karak
finger

턱 t'ək
chin

손톱 son t'op
fingernail

24

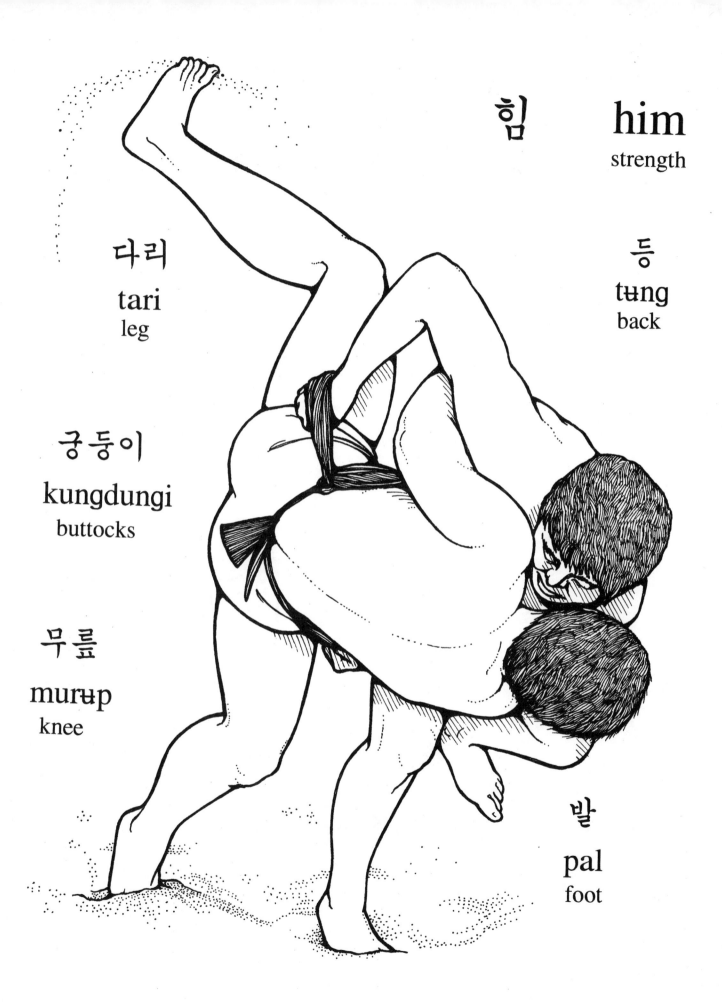

힘 him
strength

다리 tari
leg

등 tʉng
back

궁둥이 kungdungi
buttocks

무릎 murʉp
knee

발 pal
foot

25

머리
məri
head

어깨
əkkæ
shoulder

가슴 kasɯm
chest

팔 p'al
arm

손 son
hand

배 pæ
stomach

배꼽
pækkop
navel

몸　mom　body

bəs

chadong-ch'a   t'ʉrək

chiha-ch'əl   kongjang

toshi   shijang

kəri   p'ara-yo

səul   sa-yo

pihæng-gi   ton

CITY

버스　　bəs　　bus

자동차　　chadong-ch'a　　car

지하철　　chiha-ch'əl　　subway

도시 **toshi**
city

거리
kəri
street

서울 **səul** capital

비행기 pihæng-gi airplane

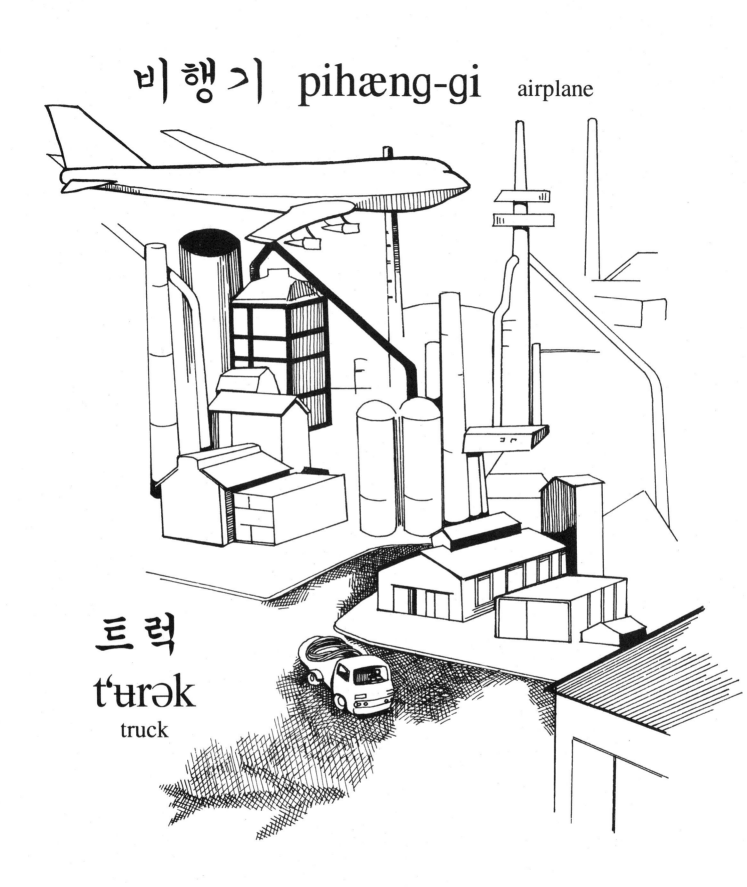

트럭
t'ʉrək
truck

공장 kongjang
factory

30

시장 shijang
marketplace

팔아요
p'ara-yo
sell

사요
sa-yo
buy

돈 ton money

ibəyo	ch'ima
korʉm	**shyassʉ**
ot	moja
kat	sʉk'ət'ʉ
chəgori	kudu
paji	yangmal

CLOTHING

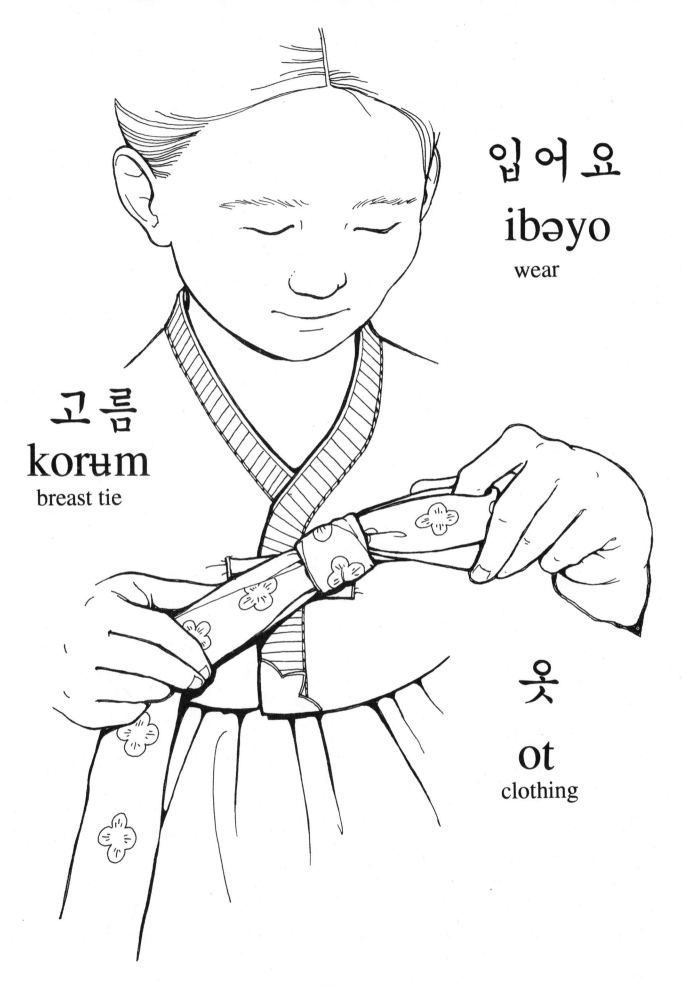

입어요
ibəyo
wear

고름
korʉm
breast tie

옷
ot
clothing

33

갓 kat
horsehair hat

저고리
chəgori
jacket

바지
paji
trousers

치마 ch'ima
dress

34

샤쓰
shyassɥ
shirt

모자
moja
hat

스커트
sɥk'ət'ɥ
skirt

바지
paji
trousers

구두
kudu
shoe

양말
yangmal
stockings

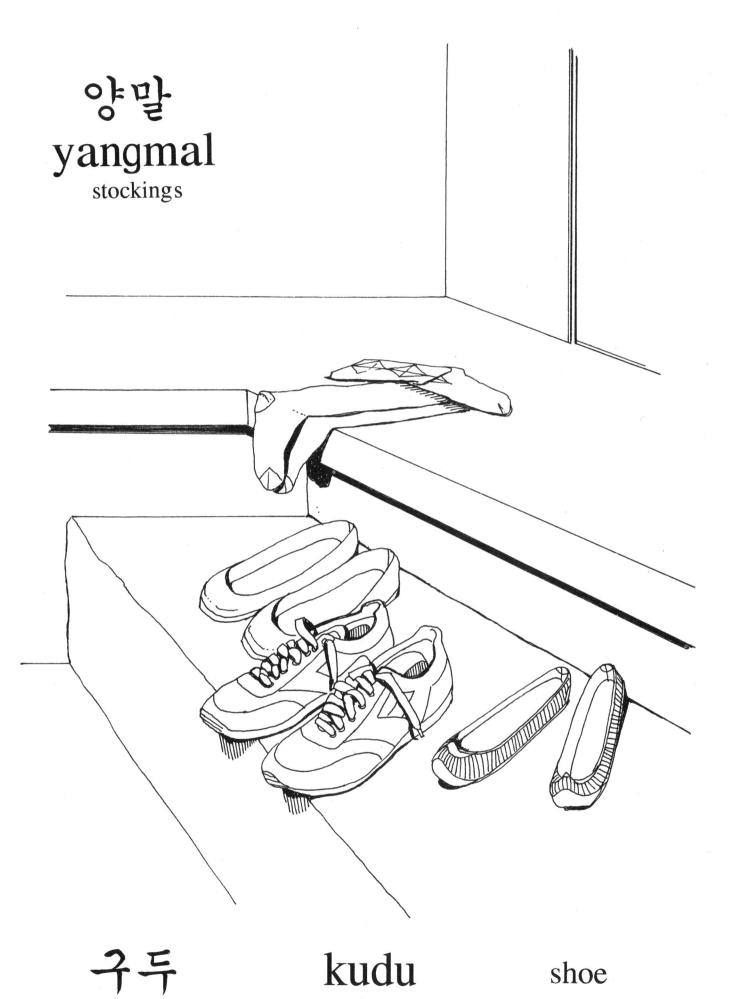

구두   kudu   shoe

kogi	ʉmshik
yuri-jan	k'al
pap	kʉrʉt
chət-karak	kimch'i
kuk	**mashyə-yo**
talgyal	məgə-yo

FOOD

고기　　　　kogi　　　meat

유리잔　　　yuri-jan
glass

밥
pap
cooked rice

국
kuk
soup

젓가락　　　chət-karak
chopsticks

달걀
talgyal
egg

38

음식 ᄈmshik
food

칼 k'al
knife

그릇
kʉrʉt
dish

김치 kimch'i
pickles

39

마셔요
mashyə-yo
drink

먹어요
məgə-yo
eat

mogyok-shil   ch'ang

nuwə-yo   chənhwa

yo   ʉija

pegæ   p'yənji

ibul   sang

pang   chip

ch'æk-sang   mun

HOME

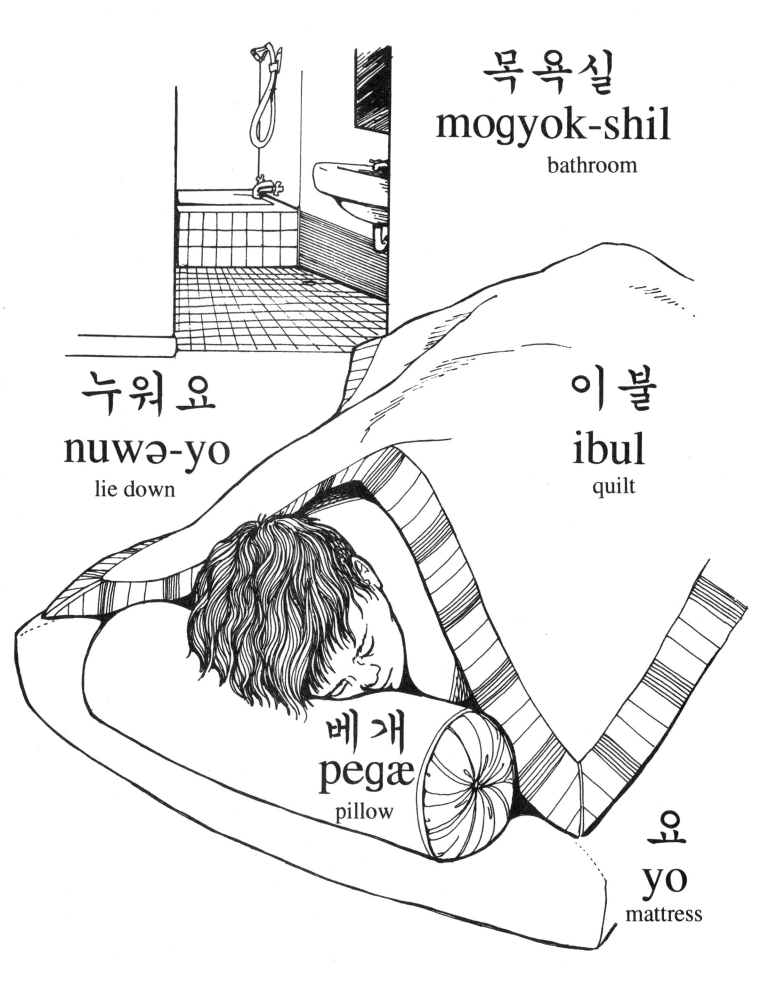

목욕실
mogyok-shil
bathroom

누워요
nuwə-yo
lie down

이불
ibul
quilt

베개
pegæ
pillow

요
yo
mattress

방 pang room

책상
ch'æk-sang
desk

창 ch'ang
window

전화
chənhwa
telephone

의자
ɰija
chair

편지
p'yənji
letter

상 sang
table

집
chip
house

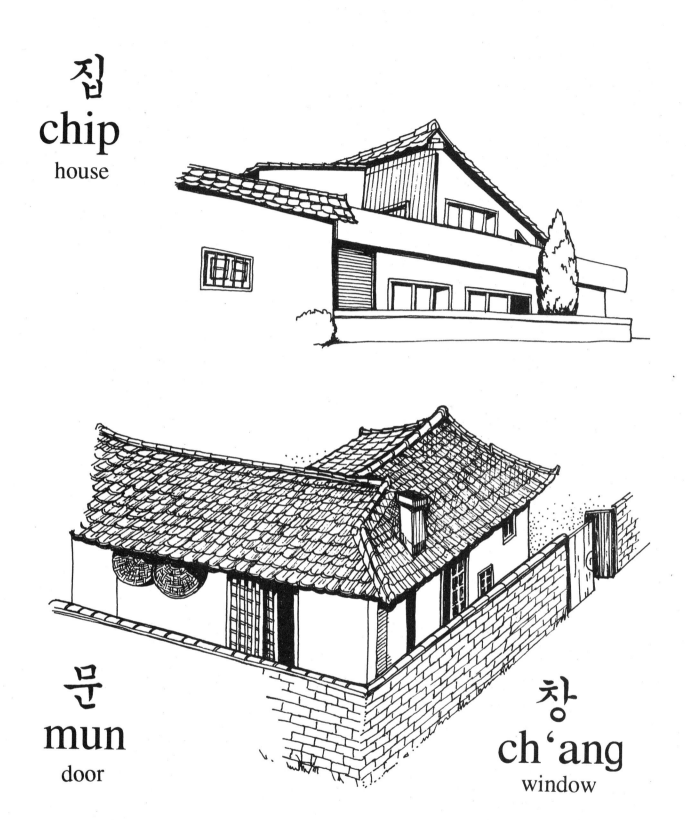

문
mun
door

창
ch'ang
window

yəp

wi

aræ

ap

kaunde

twi

mit

an

pak

kkʉt

LOCATION

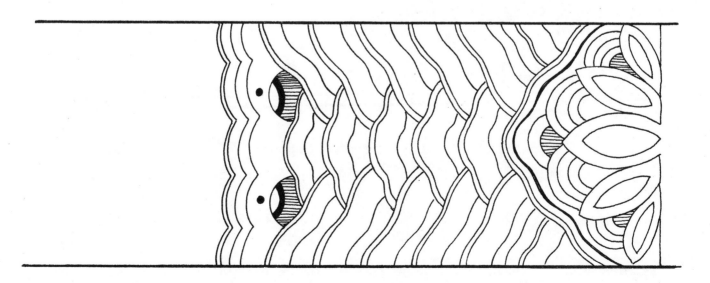

옆　　　　yəp

beside

46

위 wi

above

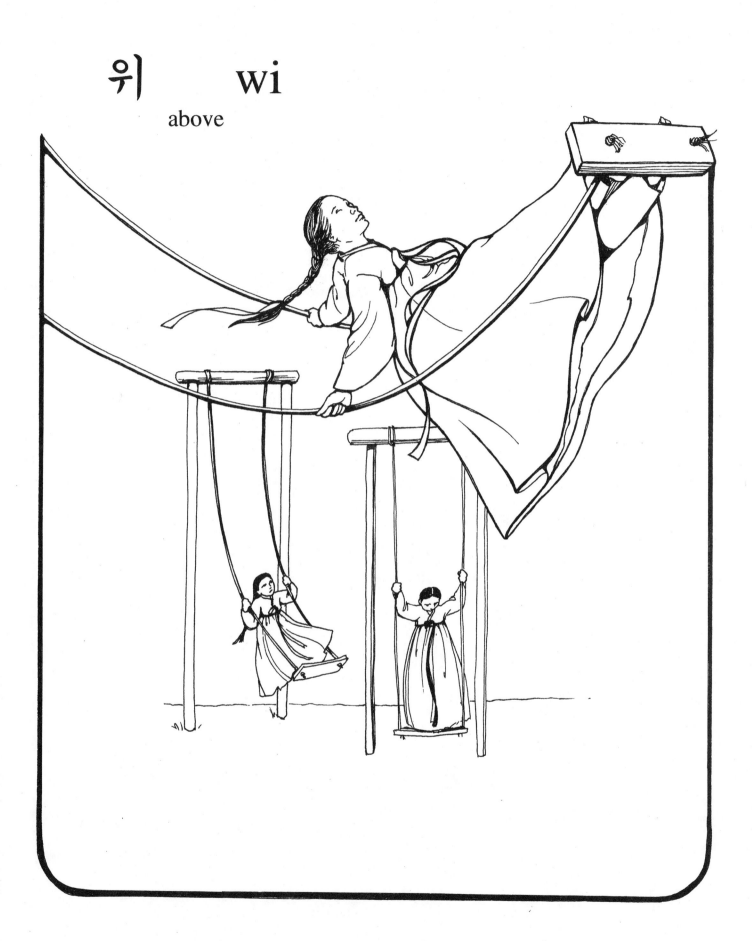

아래   aræ

beneath

앞
ap
front

가운데
kaunde
middle

뒤
twi
back

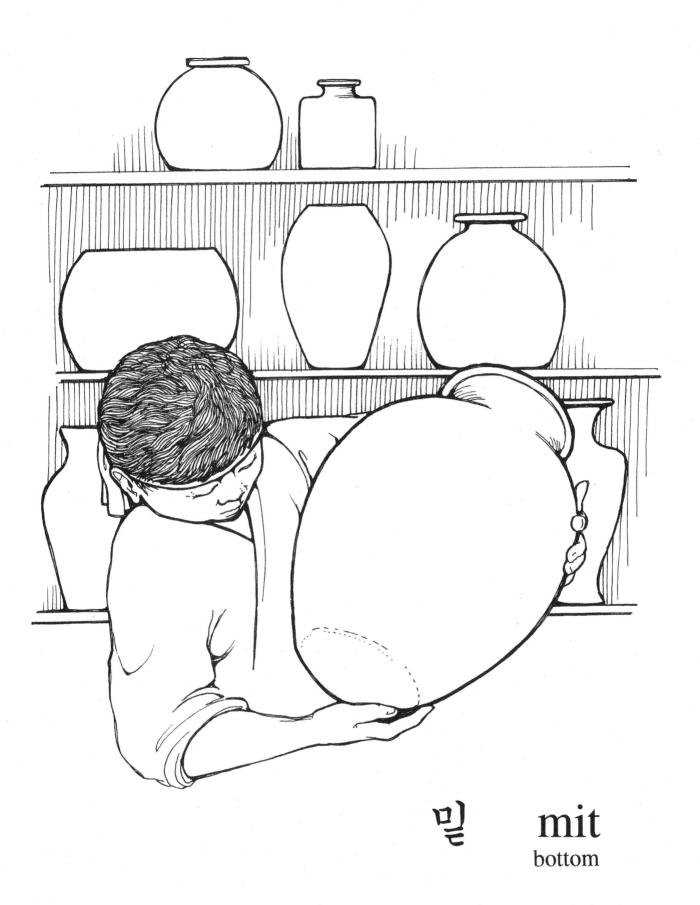

밑   mit
bottom

안
an
inside

밖
pak
outside

끝 kkʉt end

pat	nun	sə
non	ch'uwə-yo	tong
hɯk	kurɯm	nam
mal	pi	kang
kæ	san	səm
tak	pawi	pada
so	ttang	hæ
nalgæ	kil	pyəl
sæ	namu	chigu
mul kogi	kaji	tal
mul	ip	
kkot	ppuri	
hanɯl	ssi	
param	puk	

NATURE

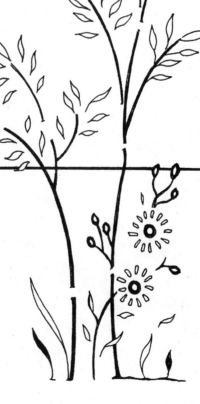

밭 pat field

논
non
paddy

흙 hʉk soil

말
mal
horse

개
kæ
dog

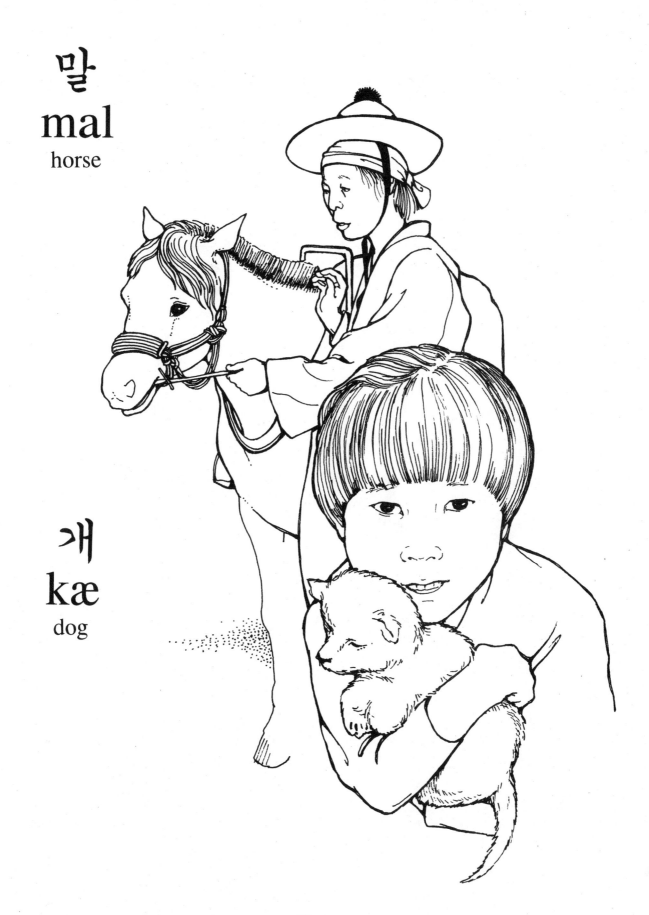

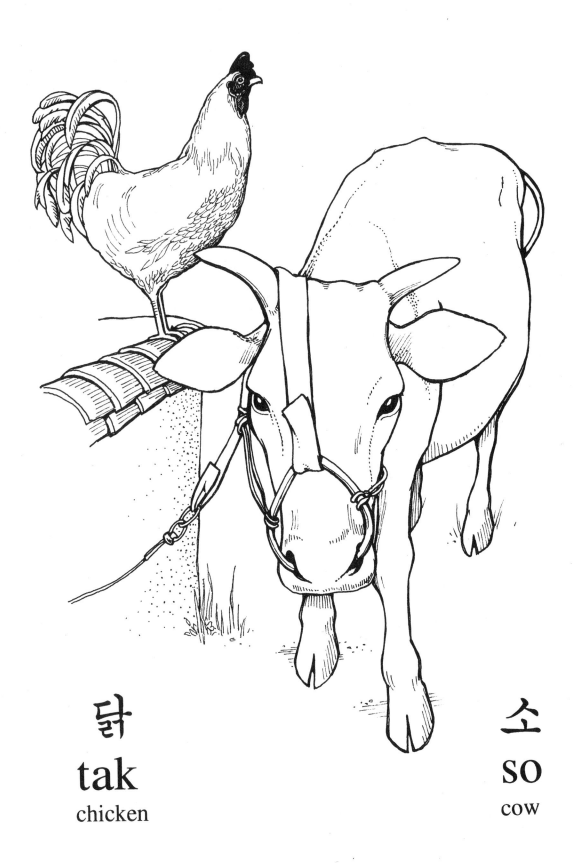

닭
tak
chicken

소
so
cow

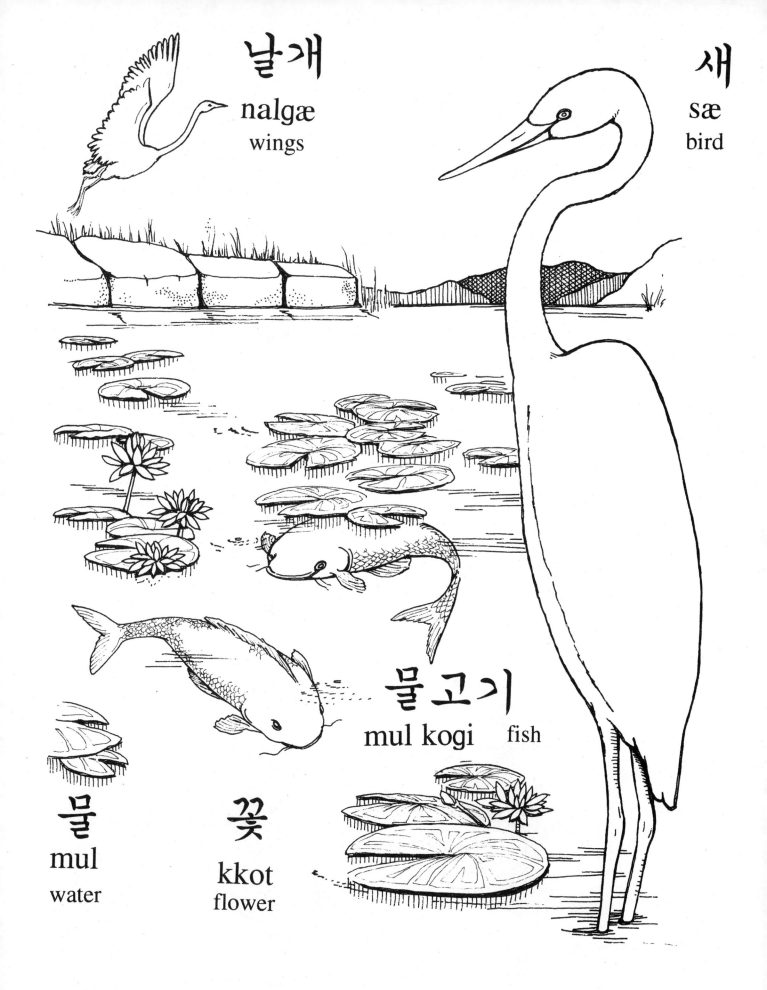

날개
nalgæ
wings

새
sæ
bird

물고기
mul kogi   fish

물
mul
water

꽃
kkot
flower

하늘
hanɨl
sky

바람
param
wind

눈
nun
snow

추워요
ch'uwə-yo   cold

58

구름   kurɐm   cloud

비   pi   rain

산 **san**
mountain

바위 **pawi**
rock

땅 **ttang**
land

길 **kil**
road

60

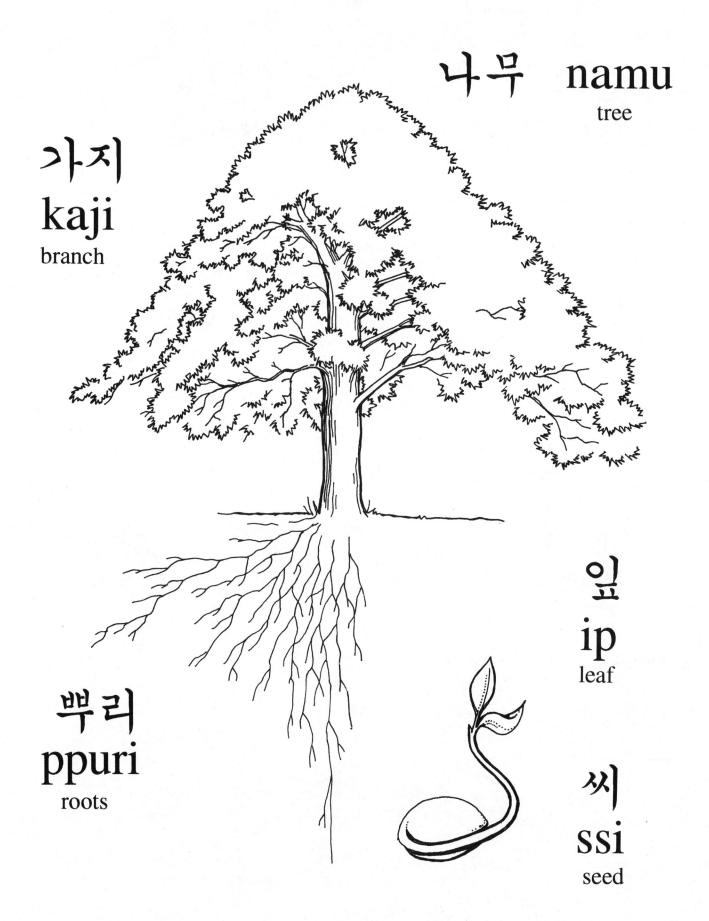

나무 namu
tree

가지
kaji
branch

잎
ip
leaf

뿌리
ppuri
roots

씨
ssi
seed

61

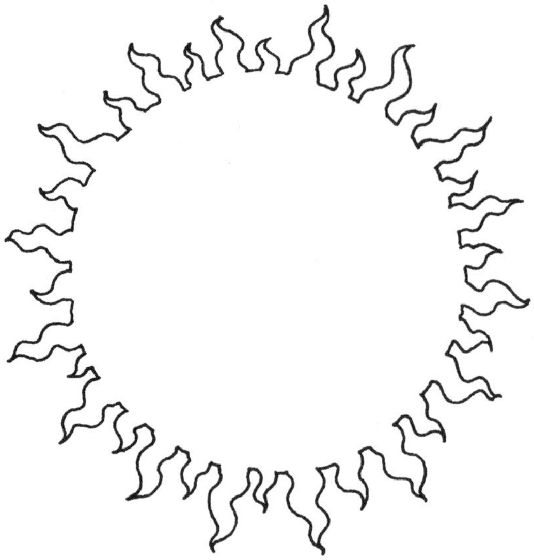

해 hæ
sun

별
pyəl
star

지구
chigu
Earth

달
tal
moon

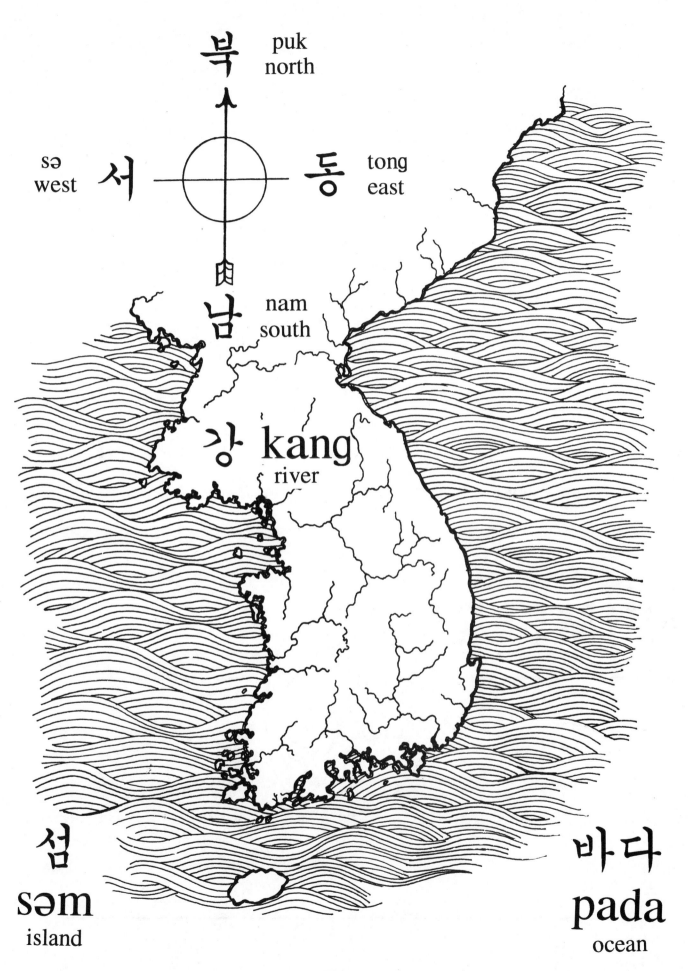

북 puk north

서 sə west

동 tong east

남 nam south

강 kang river

섬 səm island

바다 pada ocean

hana

tul   yəl

set   yəl-hana

net   yəl-tul

tasət   chero

yəsət   sumul

ilgop   sərun

yədəl   pæk

ahop   ch'ən

NUMBERS

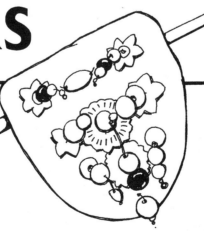

64

하나
hana
one

둘
tul
two

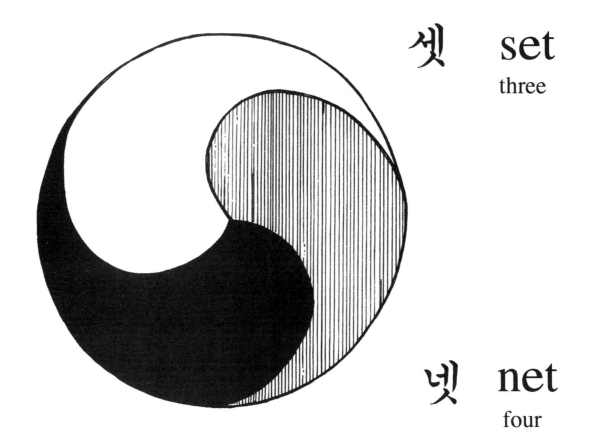

셋　set
three

넷　net
four

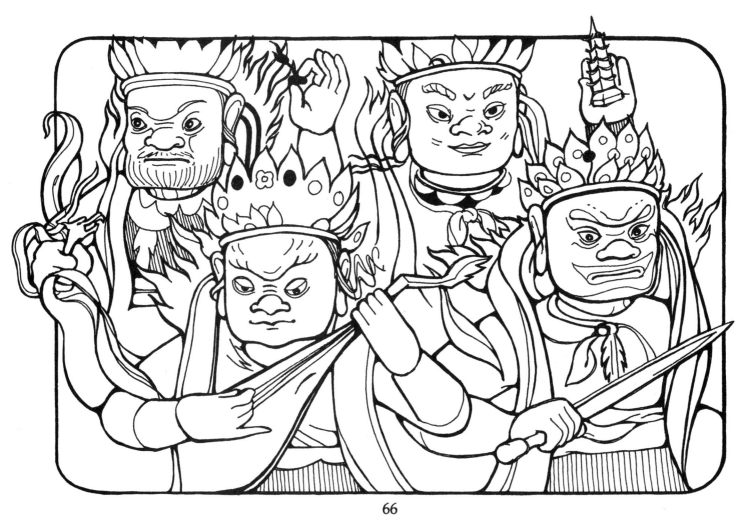

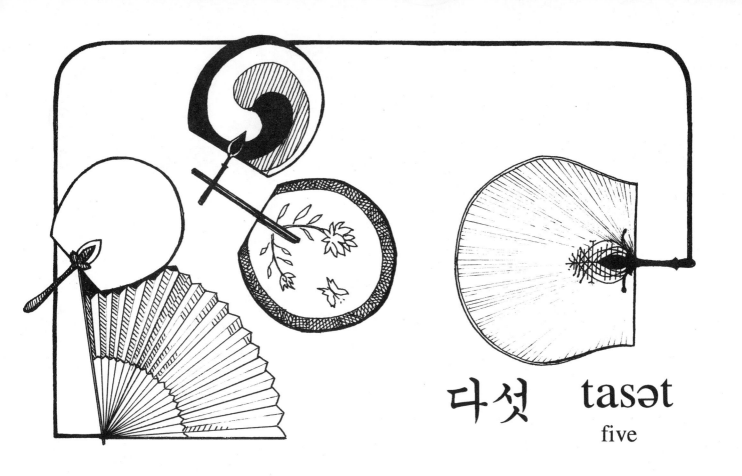

다섯 tasət
five

여섯 yəsət
six

일곱 ilgop

seven

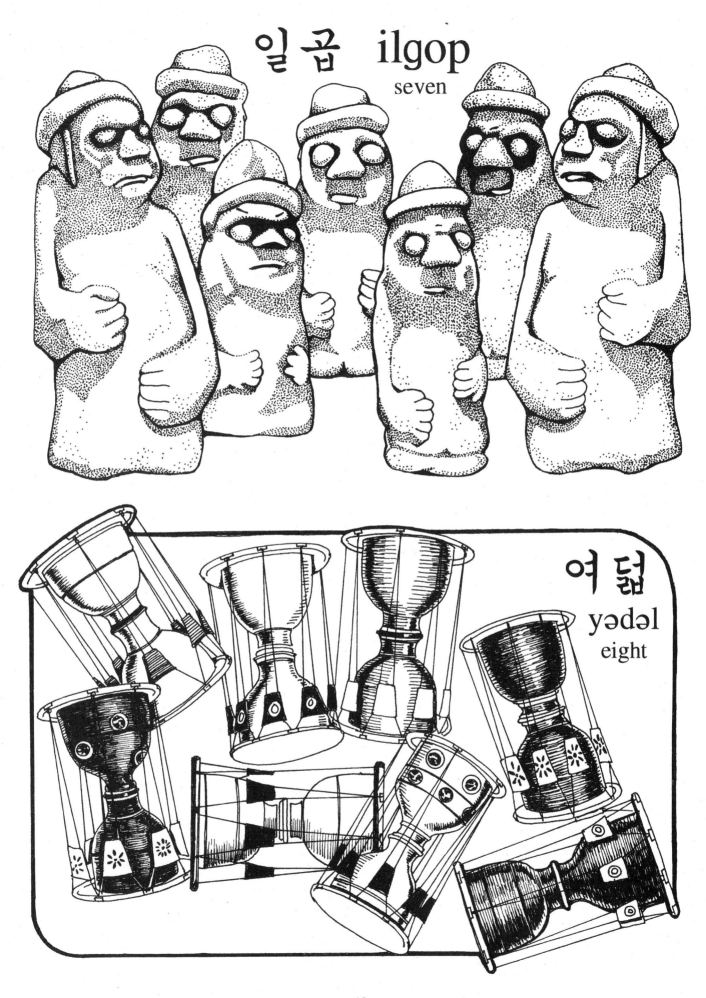

여덟

yədəl

eight

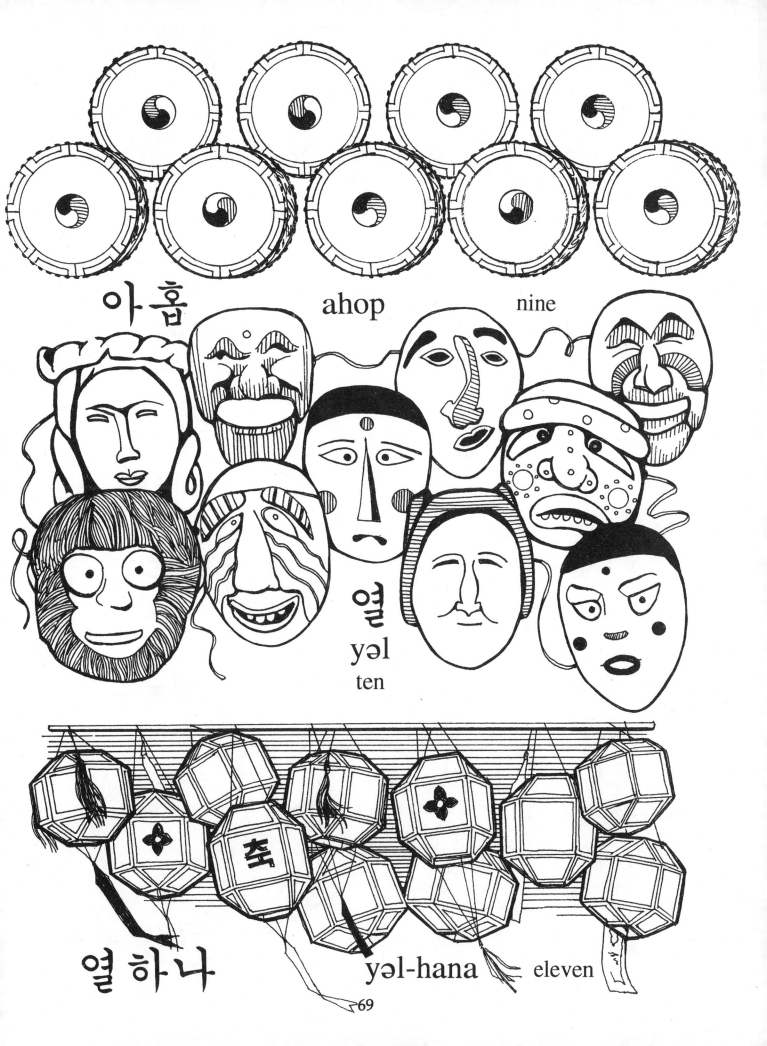

아홉   ahop   nine

열
yəl
ten

열 하나   yəl-hana   eleven

열둘　　yəl-tul　　twelve

0   영 (yəng), 공 (kong)   zero

20   스물   sʉmul   twenty

30   서른   sərʉn   thirty

100   백   pæk   hundred

1000   천   ch'ən   thousand

nʉlgə-yo   naja-yo

chəlmə-yo   mana-yo

kulgə-yo   chəgə-yo

kanʉrə-yo   mugəwə-yo

nəlbə-yo   kabyəwə-yo

choba-yo   k'ə-yo

yat'a-yo   chaga-yo

kip'ə-yo   tchalba-yo

nop'a-yo   kirə-yo

OPPOSITES

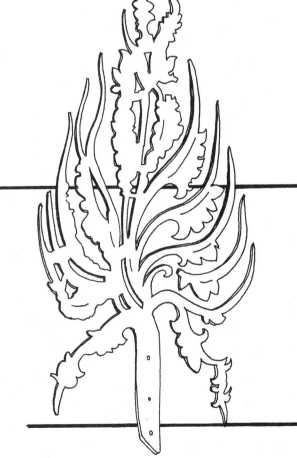

늙어요
nɯlgə-yo
old

젊어요
chəlmə-yo
young

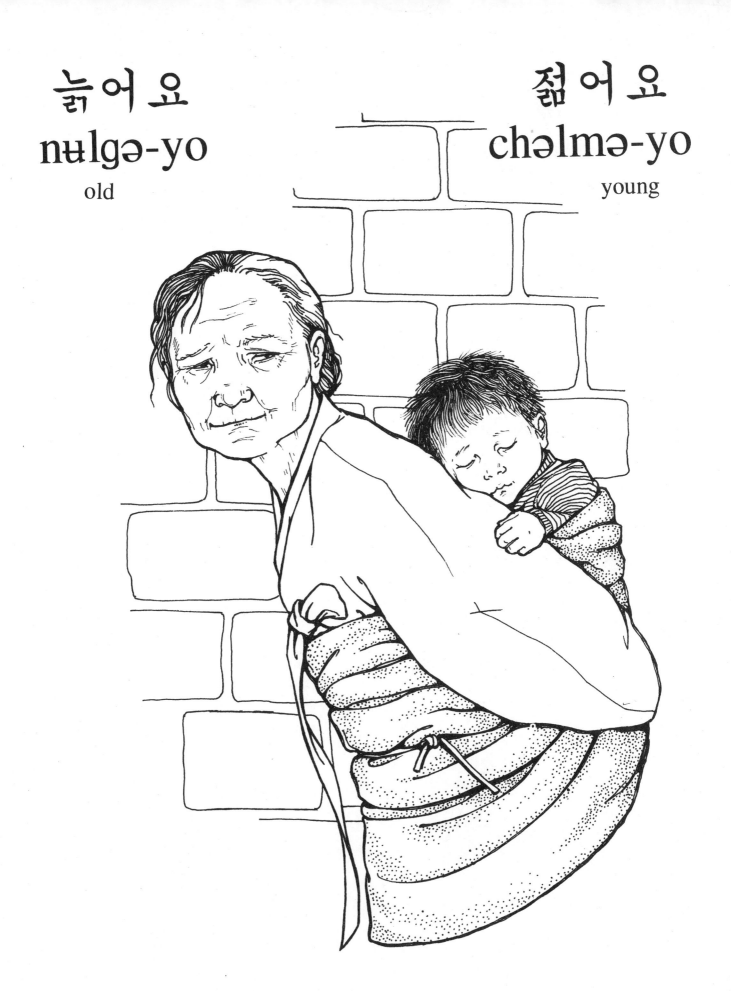

73

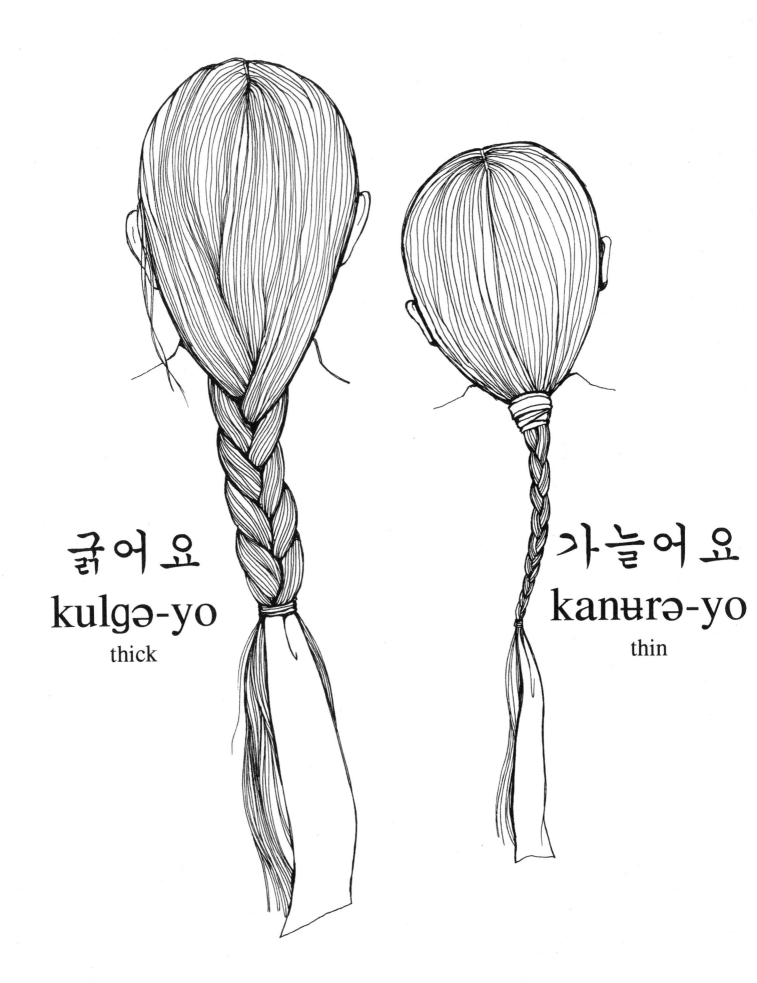

굵어요
kulgə-yo
thick

가늘어요
kanɨrə-yo
thin

넓어요　　　nəlbə-yo

wide

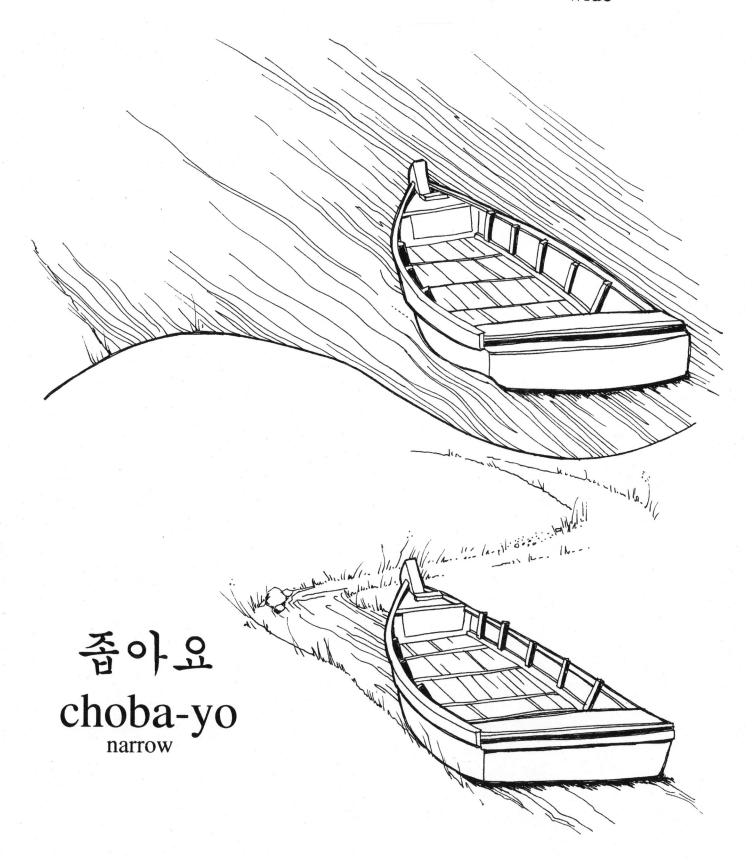

좁아요

choba-yo

narrow

얕아요 yatʻa-yo
shallow

깊어요 kipʻə-yo
deep

높아요 nop'a-yo
high

낮아요
naja-yo
low

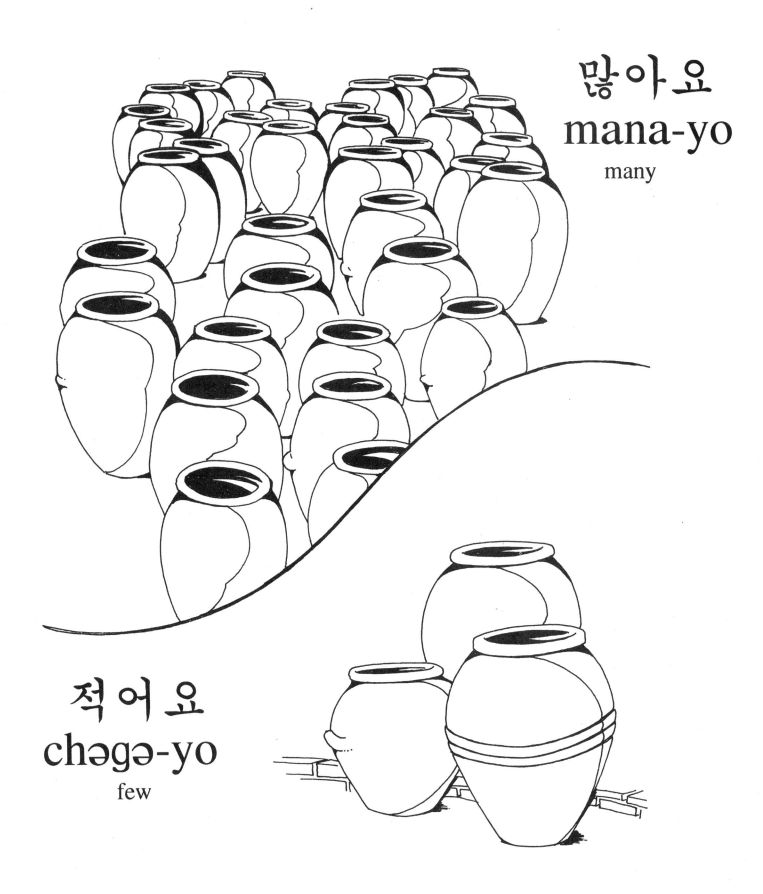

많아요
mana-yo

many

적어요
chəgə-yo

few

78

무거워요

mugəwə-yo

heavy

가벼워요

kabyəwə-yo

light

79

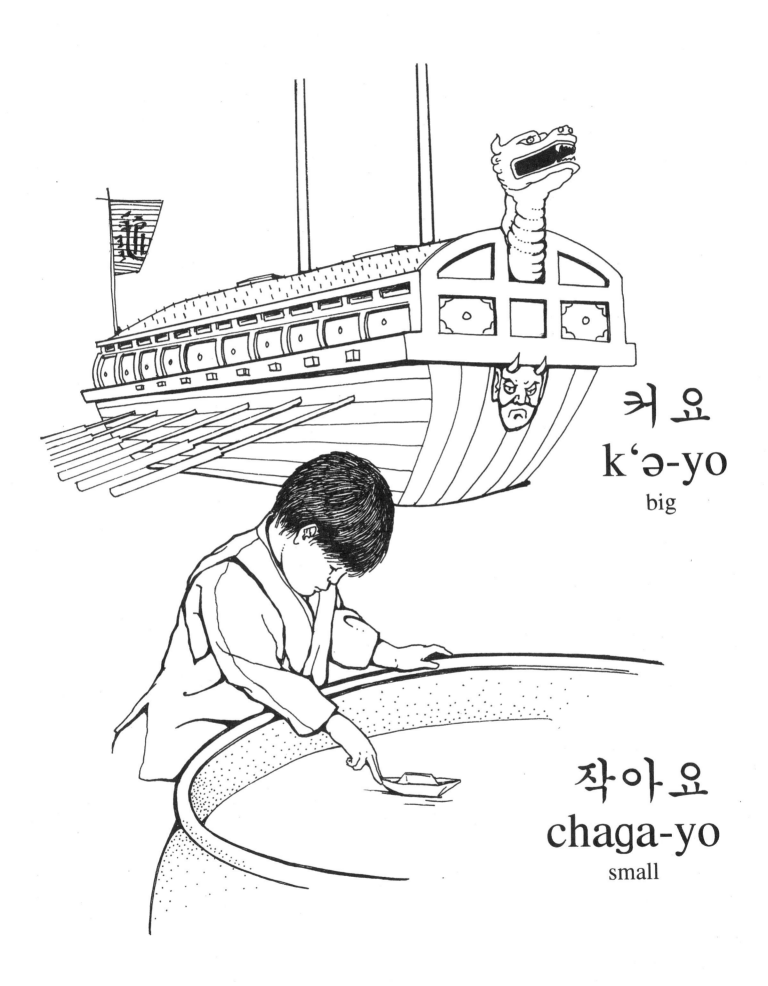

커요
k'ə-yo
big

작아요
chaga-yo
small

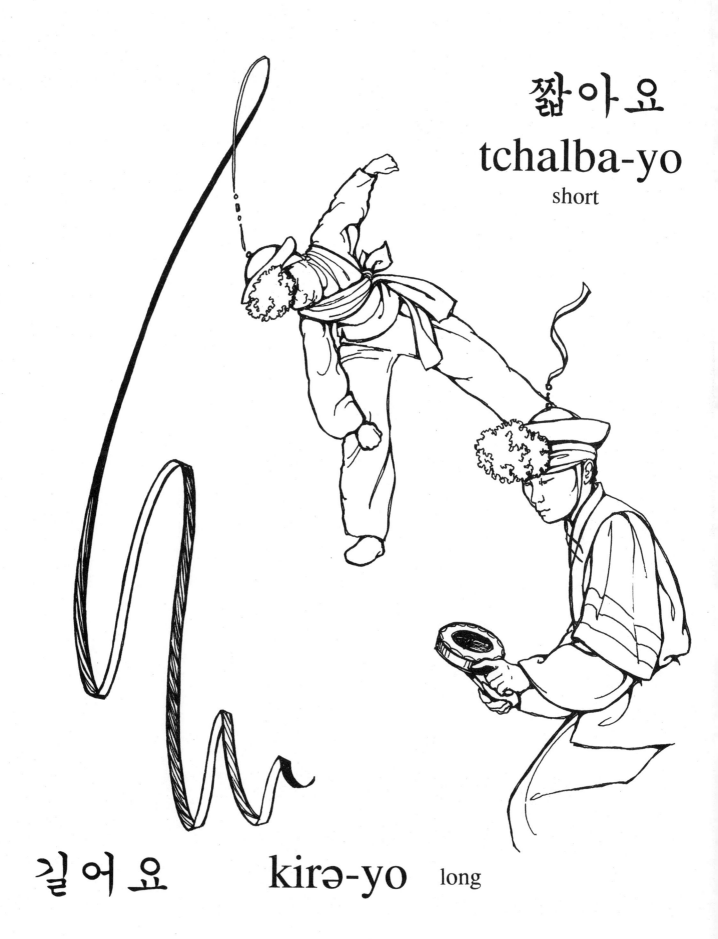

짧아요
tchalba-yo
short

길어요 kirə-yo long

harabəji	sonyə
halməni	adɰl
abəji	sonyən
namja	saram
əməni	na
yəja	chagi
pumo	irɰm
kajəng	uri
ttal	agi

PEOPLE

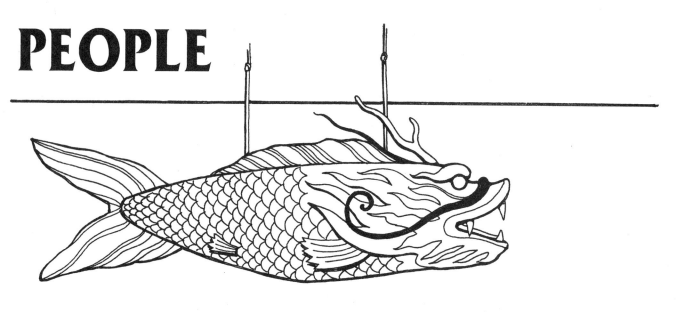

할아버지 harabəji
grandfather

할머니
halməni
grandmother

아버지 abəji
father

남자 namja
man

어머니
əməni
mother

여자
yəja
woman

부모
pumo
parents

84

가정 kajəng
family

딸
ttal
daughter

소녀
sonyə
girl

아들
adɯl
son

소년 sonyən
boy

나
na
I

사람
saram
person

자기
chagi
self

이름
irʉm
name

우리　uri
we

아기 　　　agi
baby

karʉch'yə-yo

chido	punp'il
sənsæng	ch'æk
haksæng	chiugæ
pæwə-yo	chongi
hakkyo	p'en
undong	yənp'il
noræ	iyagi
hʉkp'an	kʉrim

SCHOOL

가르쳐요   karɯch'yə-yo   teach

지도
chido
map

선생
sənsæng
teacher

학생
haksæng
student

배워요   pæwə-yo   learn

학교 hakkyo
school

운동
undong
sports

노래
noræ
song

90

흑판 hʉkpʻan
blackboard

책 chʻæk
book

분필 punpʻil
chalk

지우개 chiugæ
eraser

종이 chongi
paper

펜 pʻen
pen

연필 yənpʻil
pencil

$\mathcal{L}$ong ago and far away there lived a poor farmer who

이야기
iyagi
story

그림
kʉrim
picture